Emil's Pranks

Emil's

ILLUSTRATED BY BJORN BERG

Pranks

Astrid Lindgren

FOLLETT PUBLISHING COMPANY

CHICAGO

ISBN 0 695-40158-0 Titan binding
ISBN 0 695-80158-9 Trade binding

Library of Congress Catalog Card Number: 75-118959

Second Printing

Emil's Pranks

Perhaps you will have already heard of Emil, who lived at Katthult in Lönneberga in Småland. You haven't? Well, well! But I can assure you there isn't a single person in Lönneberga who hasn't heard of that naughty little boy. He got into more kinds of mischief than there were days in the year, and frightened the people of the district so much that they wanted to send him far away from Sweden. They did, really! They collected a lot of money and took it to his mother and said, "Maybe there's enough there to pay for sending Emil to America."

7

They thought Lönneberga would be far more peaceful without Emil, and of course that was true, but Emil's mother was very angry indeed and flung the money all over the place.

"Emil's a dear little boy," she said. "And we love him just as he is."

And Lina, the maidservant in Katthult, said, "Besides, we ought to consider the Americans, too. They've never done us any harm; so why should we plague them with Emil?"

Then Emil's mother gave her a long, severe look, and Lina realized she had said something foolish. She began stammering and tried to mend matters.

"Yes, but, madam," she said, "in the paper it reported that terrible earthquake over in America—I mean, it would be the last straw for them to have Emil on top of that!"

"Be quiet, Lina," said Emil's mother. "Go out to the byre and do the milking; that's something you *do* understand."

So Lina took the pail and ambled off to the barn. She sat down, and the cow's milk began to spurt loudly into the pail. She always worked best when she was rather annoyed, so now she milked harder than usual, muttering to her-

8

self, "There's a lot in what I said, anyway. Americans oughtn't to have still more trouble. All the same, I'd willingly change places with them, so I think I'll write to them and say, 'Here's Emil. Now send us that earthquake of yours in exchange.' "

It was just like Lina to go on about writing to America, considering that she couldn't even write a proper letter to her own folk in Småland. No, if anyone had wanted to write to America it should have been Emil's mother, who was good

at writing. She recorded all Emil's misdeeds in a blue exercise book which she kept in the drawer of her desk.

"What's the good of that?" asked Emil's father. "You'll wear out our pen if you write down all the mischief that youngster gets into."

Emil's mother took no notice, but faithfully recorded all the scrapes Emil got into so that when he grew up he would understand why she had become gray-haired. Then perhaps he would love her all the more, since it was his childhood pranks that had caused it.

Now you mustn't think Emil was horrid; no indeed. His mother was quite right when she said he was a dear little boy, and he looked like

an angel with his curly fair hair and innocent blue eyes. His mother wrote in her exercise book on July 27: "Emil was good today. He didn't get into mischief all day long, owing to the fact that he had a high temperature and couldn't get out of bed."

But by July 28 his fever had gone down so much that his doings filled several pages of his mother's book. Whenever he was well, he was strong as a young ox, and he managed to get into as much mischief as ever.

"I never saw such a child," said Lina.

You may have guessed that Lina didn't much care for Emil. She was fonder of Ida, his little sister, who was a good, obedient child.

Alfred, the farmhand, liked Emil—goodness knows why, and Emil liked him.

They had great fun together when Alfred's work was done, and he taught Emil all sorts of useful things: how to harness a horse, how to catch perch, and how to chew tobacco. Of course, tobacco chewing wasn't particularly useful, and Emil tried it only once. But he did try it, for he wanted to be able to do everything that Alfred could do. Alfred had made him a gun, and that was Emil's dearest treasure. His second dearest possession was a peaked cap which his father had bought him once when he was in the town and didn't quite realize what he was doing.

"I love my gun and my cap," Emil would say, and he never went to bed without having them beside him.

Now, do you remember who lived in Katthult? There was Emil's father, whose name was Anton; his mother, who was called Alma; his sister Ida; the farmhand Alfred; the maidservant Lina; and Emil, whose name was Emil.

And Krösa-Maja, of course, we mustn't forget her. She was a little skinny peasant woman who lived in a croft in the wood, and who was often at Katthult helping with the washing, sausage-making, and other similar tasks. She would scare Emil and Ida with stories of werewolves, ghosts, hobgoblins, murderers, robbers, and other pleasant things of which she had had experience.

But now perhaps you may like to hear something about the mischief Emil got into. He got into mischief every day except when he had a temperature, so we can choose any day at random. Let us take July 28, for instance.

SATURDAY THE TWENTY-EIGHTH OF JULY, WHEN EMIL UPSET THE BOWL OF BLOOD PUDDING OVER HIS FATHER, AND CARVED HIS ONE-HUNDREDTH LITTLE WOODEN MAN

There was an old wooden bed in the Katthult kitchen, on which Lina slept. In those days Småland was full of old beds in kitchens, where maidservants slept on knobby mattresses, with flies buzzing all around them. So why shouldn't it have been the case in Katthult, as well? Lina slept soundly on her bed. Nothing could rouse her before half past four in the morning, when the alarm clock woke her and she had to get up and go do the milking.

As soon as she left the kitchen, Emil's father used to go there and drink his morning

15

coffee in peace and quiet, before Emil woke up. He thought it delightful to sit alone by the big table, just listening to the birds singing and hearing the hens cackling as he sipped his coffee, rocking his chair a little and feeling the beautiful floorboards beneath his feet, which Lina had scrubbed until they were quite white—NO, it was the floorboards she had scrubbed, of course, not Emil's father's feet, though perhaps they could have done with a bit of a scrub, for all I know. Emil's father went barefoot in the morning, but only because it felt nice.

"A chap might as well save a bit of shoe leather while he's at it," he would say to Emil's mother, who stubbornly refused to go barefoot. "When you wear out your shoes, we have to keep on and on buying you new ones every ten years."

"Exactly," said Emil's mother, and nothing more would be said on the subject.

I said that Lina never showed a sign of life before the alarm clock rang, but one morning she did wake up because of something else. It was on July 27, the very day that Emil had a temperature. Just imagine how horrible, at four in the morning she woke because a great rat had run across her face! She jumped up with a shriek and seized hold of a log, but the rat had already disappeared into a hole beside the log box.

Emil's father was furious when he heard about the rat.

"That's a fine thing!" he stormed. "Rats in the kitchen might eat our bread and bacon."

"And *me!*" said Lina.

"And then our bread and bacon," said Emil's father. "We'll have to keep the cat in the kitchen at night."

Emil heard about the rat, and although he was in bed with a temperature, he began planning how to catch it if the cat didn't succeed.

By ten o'clock in the evening on July 27, Emil had quite recovered from his fever and was full of energy. At that hour all the other members of the Katthult household were asleep —Emil's father and mother and little Ida in the room next to the kitchen, Lina on the kitchen

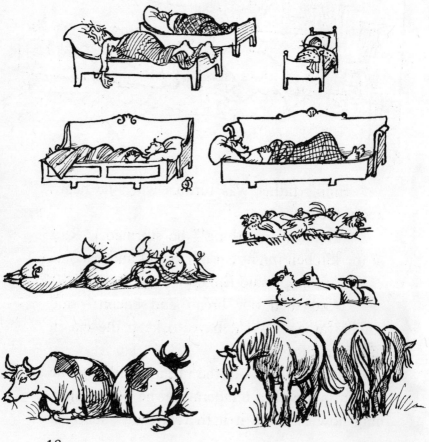

bed, and Alfred in the shepherd's cottage next
to the toolshed. Pigs and hens slept in the pig-
sty and henhouse, and the cows, horses, and
sheep slept in the green fields.

But in the kitchen the cat sat wide awake,
longing for the mice in the cowshed. Emil, too,
was wide awake, and came tip-toeing cautiously
out of the bedroom and into the kitchen.

"Poor Puss," he said, when he saw the cat
with shining eyes by the kitchen door.

"Miaow!" said the cat. And, animal lover
that he was, Emil let the cat out.

But of course he realized that the rat
must be caught, and since the cat was no longer
there, it would have to be done in some other
way. So he baited a rattrap with a nice bit of

bacon and put it near the hole by the woodbox. But then he reflected, if the rat were to see the trap the moment it put its nose out of the hole, it might be suspicious. Better let it sniff around the kitchen a bit, first, and find the trap while doing so. He thought about putting the trap on Lina's face, since that was where the rat had run, but he was afraid Lina might wake and spoil everything. No, it would have to be put elsewhere. Why not under the big table? That would be just where a rat was sure to go and hunt for crumbs—not under his father's chair, of course, since his father never dropped any crumbs.

"But suppose," he said to himself, stopping short in the middle of the kitchen floor, "suppose the rat did go there and didn't find any crumbs and began chewing Father's big toe instead!"

That would never do; he must prevent that at all costs. So he put the trap exactly where his father's feet would be, and went back to bed very pleased with himself.

He woke in broad daylight, to the sound of a loud yell from the kitchen.

"They're shouting for joy that the rat's been caught," he told himself.

The next moment his mother came hurrying in. She pulled him out of bed and hissed into his ear, "Quick! Off to the toolshed with you before your father gets his toe out of the rattrap, or I believe your last hour has come!"

And she seized Emil's hand and rushed off with him, in just his nightshirt, for there wasn't time for him to get dressed.

"But I must have my cap and gun," screamed Emil. He grabbed them and then tore off to the toolshed, his shirttails fluttering.

The toolshed was where he was sent when he had got into mischief. His mother bolted the door from outside, so that he couldn't get out, and Emil bolted it from inside so that his father couldn't get in, both of them equally prudent. Emil's mother thought it best for him not to meet his father for an hour or two, and Emil agreed.

After bolting the door securely, he sat quietly on the chopping block and began carving one of his funny little men. He used to do this whenever he was locked in the toolshed for getting into mischief, and he had already carved ninety-seven. They were neatly arranged on a shelf, and Emil liked looking at them and thinking that he would soon have one hundred. That would be quite a festive occasion. "But I shall only invite Alfred," he decided, as he sat on the chopping block, knife in hand.

He heard his father bellowing in the distance, but the noise gradually died down. Instead, there was the sound of a higher, much more piercing shriek, and Emil wondered uneasily what was wrong with his mother. But then he remembered that they were to kill the big sow that day, and that was the cause of the shrieking. Poor sow! July 28 wasn't a happy day for her. In fact, there were several for whom the day was to prove far from pleasant.

Emil was released at midday, and when he came into the kitchen, Ida ran towards him, beaming.

"We're going to have blood pudding for dinner," she said.

Perhaps you don't know what that is. It is big black lumps full of fat pork. It tastes rather like black pudding only much nicer. Emil's mother had mixed the fat and blood in a large earthenware bowl which was standing on the table, and the pot of water was already boiling in the great iron stove. There would be enough blood pudding for a real feast.

"I shall eat twenty pieces," said Ida, grandly, though she was a mite of a thing who couldn't possibly manage more than half a piece.

"Father won't let you," said Emil. "By the way, where is he?"

"He's resting," said Ida.

Emil looked out the window. Sure enough, his father was lying on the grass just outside, his straw hat over his face, having a

midday snooze as he generally did. Usually he waited till after dinner, but he was especially tired today—probably because he had begun the day in a rattrap.

Emil saw that his father was wearing only his right shoe. At first he hoped his father had decided to save shoe leather by wearing only one shoe at a time. But then he saw the blood-stained rag on his left big toe, and understood. Emil felt ashamed. His father's foot hurt so much that he couldn't bear to wear a shoe. Emil regretted his silly trick with the rattrap. He wanted to cheer his father up, and knowing that he liked blood pudding better than anything else, he took up the bowl and held it out through the window.

"Look, Papa!" he cried, joyfully. "We're having blood pudding for dinner!"

His father removed the straw hat and looked up at Emil balefully. Obviously he hadn't forgotten the rattrap, and Emil tried even harder to mend matters.

"Look what—lots of pudding!" he cried cheerfully, holding the dish out a bit farther. But just imagine how unlucky! He lost his grip on the bowl, which slipped out of his hands and tipped its gory contents all over his father as he lay on the grass!

"Blurp!" said his father, for there isn't anything else one can say when one is drenched in blood pudding mixture. But he rose heavily from the grass and let out a bellow, muffled at first by blood pudding, but becoming audible over the whole of Lönneberga. The bowl sat

like a Viking's helmet on his head, and the blood dripped down his body. Just then Krösa-Maja came from the brewhouse where she had been scalding the pig, and she saw Emil's father bathed in blood. She shrieked louder than the pig when it was being killed, and rushed away to spread the terrible news.

"Oh, oh, oh, our poor dear friend, the master of Katthult!" she screamed. "He's smothered in blood, Emil's killed him, he's done for! Oh, oh, oh!"

But when Emil's mother saw what had happened, she grabbed Emil's hand and rushed off to the toolshed once more. And while he was carving his ninety-ninth little man, she was having a tough job trying to get his father clean again.

"You may be able to scrape off enough to make three or four sausages, anyway," said Emil's father.

But she shook her head. "What's been spilt stays spilt," she said. "We'll have to eat fritters instead."

"Hee hee!" giggled little Ida. "We shan't have any dinner till suppertime." But she grew silent, for she saw her father's gloomy expression through the blood pudding mixture.

Emil's mother asked Lina to slice potatoes for the fritters. I can assure you that potato fritters taste a great deal better than you may think. Soon Lina had beaten up a thick grayish yellow batter in the bowl Emil's father had removed from his head. He didn't want to go around looking like a Viking all day. As soon as he was fairly clean again, he went to the fields to start cutting the rye, and to wait for the fritters to be prepared. Only then did Emil's mother let him out of the toolshed.

Emil had been sitting still a long time. Now he felt it was time to move about a bit.

"We'll play Got You!" he told little Ida, and she ran off at once.

Got You! was a running game Emil had

invented. You had to run for dear life, from the kitchen to the front door and from there to the back room and back to the kitchen again and from there to the front door, round and round until you couldn't run any more. Emil and Ida each went off in a different direction, and every time they met they jabbed each other in the stomach and shouted, "Got you!" which was why the game got its name, and both children thought it tremendous fun.

But when on the eighty-eighth circuit Emil came rushing into the kitchen, he met Lina, carrying the bowl of batter, on her way to the stove to start frying the fritters. He wanted

to give her a bit of fun too; so he jabbed her in the stomach and shouted, "Got you!" He oughtn't to have done that, for he knew how ticklish Lina was.

"Eeee!" squealed Lina, writhing like a worm. And just fancy how dreadful—the bowl flew out of her hands. Nobody knew exactly how it happened. The only thing certain is that Emil's father, ravenous with hunger, was coming through the door and the batter splashed all over him!

"Blurp!" he said again—for you can't say anything else when your face is smothered with batter.

Emil and Ida used it as a favorite expression of theirs afterwards. " 'Blurp,' as Papa said in the batter," they would say, giggling, or " 'Blurp,' as Papa said in the blood pudding," which sounded just as funny.

But at that moment Emil hadn't time to giggle, for his mother seized his hand and rushed him off to the toolshed again. Behind him Emil heard his father's bellowings, muted by batter at first, but then audible all over Lönneberga.

As Emil sat carving his one-hundredth little man, he was far from being in a good temper. Quite the contrary, he was as angry as a red ant! It was a bit too much, sitting in the toolshed three times in one day, he considered, and unfair besides.

"Is it my fault that Papa keeps getting in the way everywhere?" he fumed. "You can't so much as set a rattrap without him blundering into it. And why has he got to turn up just as blood pudding and batter are flying about?"

Now I wouldn't for the world have you imagine that Emil wasn't fond of his father or that his father wasn't fond of Emil. They were excellent friends ordinarily, but even affectionate people occasionally fall out when misfortunes happen.

Saturday, July 28 drew to a close. Emil sat in the toolshed getting angrier and angrier about everything and everybody. This wasn't how he had imagined celebrating the creation of his one-hundredth little carved man. For one thing, it was Saturday evening and how could he invite Alfred to a feast in the toolshed? Alfred had other things to do on Saturday evenings. He usually sat on the back door step canoodling with Lina and playing the concertina for her. He certainly hadn't time for a party.

Emil flung aside his knife. He didn't even have Alfred; he was all alone and growing more and more enraged at the way people treated him. Was it right that he should be sitting there wearing only a nightshirt, all through an endless Saturday, not even having time to put on any clothes because of this everlasting rushing out to the toolshed? But since they wanted him to be there, very well! They would have their wish. He banged his fist on the bench with a

crash. Yes, they would have their way. At that
moment he reached a terrible decision. He
would remain in the toolshed for the rest of his
days, wearing only his nightshirt and his cap,
alone and forsaken by all. He would stay there
for the rest of his life.

"So they'll be satisfied at last, and there
won't have to be all this traipesing back and
forth," he said to himself. "But they needn't
think they can come into my toolshed—no indeed! And if Papa wants to cut some logs, he'll
just have to want, that's all. Which is probably
as well, because like as not he'd cut off his own

thumb. I never knew such a chap for getting himself into a mess."

But towards evening Emil's mother came and raised the latch of the toolshed, from the outside, of course. She shook the door and realized that it was bolted from inside, as well. She smiled, fondly.

"You needn't be scared any longer, Emil dear. Father's gone to sleep. You can come out now."

A grim "Ha!" sounded from inside the toolshed.

"Why do you say 'ha' like that?" she asked. "Open the door, dear, and come out."

"I'm never coming out again," said Emil, quietly. "And don't try to come in or I'll shoot you."

Emil's mother saw him at the window, gun in hand. At first she didn't believe he was serious, but when she realized he was, she burst into tears and ran to wake his father.

"Emil's in the toolshed and won't come out," she sobbed. "What are we to do?"

Little Ida woke up, too, and started howling at once. And they all ran off to the toolshed. So did Alfred and Lina, who had been

courting by the back door, and who, much to Lina's fury, had to stop doing so. Everyone had to help convince Emil to come out of the shed.

"You'll come out quick enough when you get hungry," said Emil's father.

"Ha!" said Emil once more.

His father didn't know that long ago, he had put a container behind the chopping block. Just a few emergency provisions. He had made sure he wouldn't starve—he was too smart for that. He never knew when he would be sent to the toolshed, so he always saw to it that there was something to eat in his container. Just now there was rye bread, cheese, two pieces of cold pork, lots of dried cherries, and plenty of biscuits. Prisoners have held out in beleaguered fortresses on less food than that. And Emil felt that the toolshed was a beleaguered fortress, and he meant to defend it against all his enemies. Bold as the leader of a garrison, he stood by the window, aiming his gun.

"I shall shoot the first one who moves," he shouted.

"Oh, my darling little boy, don't talk like that," sobbed his mother. But it was no good; Emil was inflexible.

It was useless even for Alfred to say, "Listen, Emil, if you come out we'll go swimming in the lake, you and I."

"No thank you," answered Emil, bitterly. "You can sit on the step with Lina, and I'll stay here."

And that was that. And when neither

threats nor entreaties proved of any use, Emil's father and mother and little Ida had to go in to bed.

It was a miserable Saturday evening. Emil's mother and little Ida wept torrents of tears, and his father sighed heavily as he got into bed. He missed his little boy.

Lina, however, didn't miss Emil at all, nor did she want to go to bed. She wanted to continue sitting peacefully with Alfred, so she was delighted that Emil remained in the toolshed.

"Though goodness knows how long the wretched child will really stay there," she said to herself, and sneaked off to the shed and bolted it again from the outside.

Alfred was playing his concertina and never noticed the horrid thing Lina had done.

"Home from the field of battle rode the Huzzar," sang Alfred. Emil, sitting on the chopping block, heard him and heaved a deep sigh.

But Lina put her arm around Alfred's neck, as she always did, and Alfred said, as he always did, "Oh well, maybe I'll marry you as you're so dead set on it, but there's no hurry."

"Well, next year, anyhow," insisted Lina, and Alfred sighed even more heavily than Emil and sang about the Lion Bride. Emil heard that, as well, from the toolshed, and began thinking what fun it would be to go down to the lake with Alfred.

"Of course," he told himself, "I could just take a turn with Alfred, have a swim, and come back to my toolshed again if I liked."

He ran to the door and unbolted it. But what was the good of that, since nasty Lina had bolted it from the outside? It wouldn't open no matter how hard he pushed. He realized at once who had locked him in.

"But I'll show her," he said. "She'll see, all right."

It had begun to get dark. He looked all around the shed. Once, after one of his worst scrapes, he had escaped through the window.

But after that his father had nailed two bits of wood across the glass from the outside, so Emil couldn't try that again.

"I can't get through the window, nor through the door," Emil said to himself. "I'll never, never call for help. What shall I do?"

He looked thoughtfully at the stove, which was open. It was put there so Emil's father could keep warm in the winter and be able to heat up his gluepot when necessary.

"It will have to be up the chimney," said Emil. And treading in the ashes left from last winter's fires, he peered up the chimney pipe and saw something delightful. Right above his head a red July moon was peeping down at him.

"Hullo, you old moon," said Emil. "Now you'll see me do a bit of climbing." And bracing his feet against the sooty sides of the chimney, he started to climb.

If you have ever tried climbing up the inside of a narrow chimney, you will know how difficult it is and how black you can get—but this didn't discourage Emil.

Poor, luckless Lina, sitting with her arm around Alfred's neck on the back door step, knew nothing about it. But Emil had said she

38

would see—and so she did. She looked up at
the moon, and then gave a yell that could be
heard all over Lönneberga.

"A howliboo!" shrieked Lina. "There's a
howliboo on the chimney!"

Howliboos are a kind of child spook that
frightened people of Småland in olden times.
Lina had heard a lot of dreadful tales about
little howliboos from Krösa-Maja, and so she
screamed when she saw one sitting on the chimney stack, coal-black and frightful to behold.

Alfred looked at the howliboo and just
laughed.

"I recognize that little howliboo," he said.
"Come down, Emil."

Emil stood there, dauntless as the leader of
a garrison, in his sooty shirt. He raised his sooty
fists and yelled, "This very evening shall the
toolshed be torn down and I shall never be
locked in it again."

Then Alfred went to stand by the gable,
just beneath Emil, and held out his arms.
"Jump!" he called. And Emil did jump, and
Alfred caught him. And then they both went
down to the lake to swim. Emil needed a bath,
anyway.

"I never saw such a child," said Lina,
bursting with rage, and she went to her bed in
the kitchen.

But Alfred and Emil swam among the
white waterlilies in the warm lake water, and up
in the sky the July moon shone for them like a
red lantern.

"You and I, Alfred," said Emil.

"Yes, Emil, you and I."

A broad, shining moonbeam glistened across the lake, but it was dark around the shore. Night had come by this time, and it was the end of July 28.

But other days were to come, and fresh mischief. Emil's mother wrote so hard in the blue notebook that she got quite a pain in her arm, and at last the book was absolutely full.

"I'll have to buy a new book," she said. "I'll do it when we go to Vimmerby Fair."

And so she did, which was just as well, for otherwise she wouldn't have had room to tell of all the mischief Emil got into on the day of the Fair.

"Heaven preserve us," she wrote, "but that boy will go far if he lives to grow up, which his father doesn't believe he will."

But Emil's father was wrong, and his mother was right.

Emil certainly did live to grow up and actually became president of the local council and the finest fellow in all Lönneberga. But we will continue with what happened at Vimmerby Fair one day when he was little.

WEDNESDAY THE THIRTY-FIRST OF OCTOBER, WHEN EMIL GOT A HORSE AND SCARED THE LIFE OUT OF MRS. PETRELL AND ALL OF VIMMERBY

Vimmerby Fair was held every year on the last Wednesday in October, and on that day there was hustle and bustle and excitement in the town from early morning till late at night, I can assure you. Everybody from Lönneberga and neighboring parishes went there to sell oxen and buy bullocks and exchange horses and meet people and find sweethearts and eat peppermints and dance the schottiche and fight and enjoy themselves, each in his own way.

Emil's mother once asked Lina if she knew which were the great festivals of the year, and

42

Lina said, "Well, there's Easter and Christmas and Vimmerby Fair."

At five o'clock in the morning, when it was dark as pitch, Alfred harnessed the two horses, Markus and Jullan, to the big waggonette and off went the whole party from Katthult, Emil's father and mother, Alfred and Lina, Emil and little Ida. Only Krösa-Maja was left behind to look after the animals.

"Poor Krösa-Maja, don't you want to come too?" asked Alfred, who was a kindly soul.

"I'm not crazy," said Krösa-Maja. "To-day, when the great comet is coming? No, thank you. I'll die at home in Lönneberga, where I belong."

Krösa-Maja was talking about the great comet that the people of Småland were expecting to fall. The *Vimmerby Herald* had written that it was due on October 31. The great rushing comet would hurtle down and perhaps crash into the earth and smash it to bits.

Probably you don't really know what a comet is, and I myself hardly know either. But I think it is part of a star which has broken apart and it goes whirling around, here, there, and all over the place. All the Småland folk were terrified at the thought of the comet which would shatter the world and put an end to everything jolly and happy.

"And of course the hateful thing *would* come just when Vimmerby Fair is on," said Lina crossly. "Still, maybe it won't come before the evening, so we'll have had time to enjoy everything first."

She gave a sly grin and nudged Alfred with her elbow as he sat beside her in the back of the waggonette. She had great expectations for this particular day.

Emil's mother sat in front with little Ida on her lap, and Emil's father sat with Emil on his knee. Guess who was driving? Emil! I forgot to say what a clever chap he was where horses were concerned. It was Alfred who had begun teaching him everything he needed to know about horses, but in the end Emil knew more about them than anyone else in Lönneberga, including Alfred. Now he sat on his father's knee and drove like any experienced coachman—oh yes, he knew how to handle the reins all right!

It had rained during the night; darkness and mist lay like a veil over Småland that chilly October morning. No light was showing over the treetops yet, and the woods stood black and rain sodden on both sides of the road as the Katthult party made its way in the waggonette. But they were all cheerful, nevertheless, and Markus and Jullan trotted so that the clay from the muddy road spurted around their hooves.

Jullan wasn't particularly happy, of course, for she was old and infirm and would rather have remained at home. For a long time Emil had been begging his father to get a young horse that would be better in harness with Markus, and the Fair offered a good opportunity to find one, he considered.

But his father said, "You seem to think I can afford anything. No, we'll have to make do with old Jullan for another couple of years; it can't be helped."

And Jullan did her best. She plodded gamely up the hills, and Emil, who loved her, sang as he usually did when he wanted to cheer her up a bit:

> *Jullan plods pluckily along,*
> *Although her legs are none too strong,*
> *And she's the worse for wear,*
> *She does her work so sturdily*
> *And bears my cap and gun and me,*
> *I love my game old mare.*

When they reached Vimmerby and had found a good place to tether Jullan and Markus not far from the cattle market, they all had different things to do. Emil's mother, with little Ida clutching at her skirt, went to buy a blue notebook, and to sell the wool and eggs she had brought to market. Lina wanted to go at once to the refreshment stall to drink coffee with Alfred. And she dragged him with her, while he jibbed and protested, because he preferred to go with Emil and Emil's father to the cattle market. The cheerful noise and bustle were in full swing there. Emil was off like a shot, and his father had no objection to going with him, although he hadn't any intention of buying anything, only of looking around.

"But remember we've been invited to lunch with Mrs. Petrell at twelve o'clock," said Emil's mother, just before disappearing with little Ida.

"You needn't be afraid I should forget such a thing as that," said Emil's father, before going off with Emil.

But Emil hadn't been five minutes at the cattle market before he caught sight of the horse! The horse he wanted, and which made his heart beat as it had never beaten before.

Such a horse! A beautiful little brown horse,
two years old. He stood tethered to a fence and
looked kindly at Emil, as though he hoped he

would buy him. And oh, how badly Emil wanted to do so! He searched for his father so he could begin pestering him and keep on and on until he absolutely *had* to buy the horse for the sake of peace. But fancy how maddening— his father had vanished! He had disappeared in the medley of peasants who shouted and laughed, and horses that neighed and stamped, and cows and bullocks that bellowed and mooed in one great hullaballoo.

It's always the same, thought Emil, bitterly. You can't take him anywhere without him disappearing the first chance he gets.

And now there was need to hurry. A horse dealer from Målilla had come along and was eyeing Emil's horse.

"What are you asking for that one?" he asked the peasant in charge of the horses, a pallid little man from Tuna. Emil's stomach turned over when he heard it cost three-hundred kronor. Getting three-hundred kronor out of his father would be like getting blood out of a stone.

I shall have a try, all the same, he thought, for he was the most stubborn youngster in all of Småland. And he set off into the crowd to find his father. He ran hither and thither, getting more desperate, pushing and tugging at everybody he thought was his father. They all looked alike from behind, but when they turned around, they were always strangers.

You needn't think Emil gave up on that account. There was a little flagpole by the fence, and in a flash Emil had climbed to the top of it so that everyone could see him, and shouted, "Does anyone here recognize me? My father has got lost!"

Then, from the surging mass of peasants and cattle and horses, somebody came hurrying toward the flagstaff. It was his father, who shook him down as if he had been a ripe apple on a tree and grabbed him by the ear.

"You wretched child, where have you been?" he asked. "Must you always disappear the moment I take my eyes off of you?"

Emil had no time to reply to this. "Come at once!" Emil said. "There is a horse you *must* see."

And Emil's father certainly did see the horse, but it was already sold! Imagine how dreadful! Emil and his father came just in time to see the horse dealer from Målilla pull out his

wallet and push three-hundred kronor into the
hand of the peasant from Tuna.

Emil burst into tears.

"That's a nice horse," said the dealer.

"Yes, he's a very good horse," agreed the
peasant. But he looked sideways as he said it,
and it seemed as if he were thinking of something.

"I see he isn't shod," said the dealer. "I'll
have to get that attended to before I start for
home."

Emil stood there crying, and his father felt
sorry for him.

"Don't cry," he said. "Come on and we'll
get you a stick of peppermint rock."

And he took Emil to the confectionery

stall and bought him ten öres' worth of striped peppermint rock. But then he met a friend from Lönneberga and forgot about Emil as they chatted together. Emil stood there with his mouth full of peppermint rock and his eyes full of tears, thinking about the horse.

And suddenly he saw Alfred, with Lina hanging onto his arm. Poor Alfred looked quite tired, which wasn't surprising, as Lina had walked him back and forth in front of the jeweller's shop seventeen times, trying to persuade him to buy an engagement ring.

"If I hadn't dug my toes in, goodness knows what might have happened," said Alfred, happily. He was glad to see Emil, of course. Emil hurriedly told him about the horse, and they stood sighing over the fact that the horse would never be coming to Katthult. But then Alfred bought Emil a clay cuckoo, from the potter who sold such things in the market.

"Here's a little present from me," he said, and at once Emil felt his grief somewhat lightened.

"Humph, so you can buy clay cuckoos," said Lina. "But how about that comet? I think it's about time it came along."

But there was no sign of the comet, and it was scarcely midday, so there wasn't any hurry.

Alfred and Lina had to go tend Markus and Jullan and have a bit of lunch. They had brought a packet of food in a box and had left it in the waggonette. Emil would have enjoyed going with them, but he knew he had to go to lunch with Mrs. Petrell at twelve, so he looked about for his father. And believe it or not, his father had disappeared again. He had got lost among the potters, basket makers, balloon sellers, and all the rest of the market crowd.

"I never saw anyone like him for getting lost," said Emil. "Next time I come to the town he'll have to stay at home. We can't go on like this."

However, it didn't worry him that his father had disappeared. He had been in the town before and knew where Mrs. Petrell lived. She had a smart little white house with a white veranda, near High Street. It oughtn't to be too hard to find it, he thought.

Mrs. Petrell was one of the grandest ladies in Vimmerby, so it was rather strange that she should invite the Katthult folk to lunch. But she was always coming over to Katthult for various parties—cherry parties, crayfish parties, cheesecake parties, and other parties where they served sausages, spareribs of pork, fillets of veal, meatballs, jellied eels, omelets, and things of that sort. You can't go on and on being a guest without sometimes returning the hospitality, thought Mrs. Petrell. So she decided on the day when the Katthult people would be in the town for the Fair, and invited them to lunch. They would have warmed-up fish pie and blueberry sauce. She herself had a meal at eleven, just a trifle of fillet of veal and a large slice of marzipan tart, since there wasn't much of the fish pie. And it wouldn't be polite for her to sit stuffing herself, if there wasn't a decent helping for each guest.

54

Now they were seated around the table in the glass veranda, Emil's father and mother and little Ida.

"That wretched child, it's easier to hold a handful of fleas than keep track of him," said Emil's father.

Emil's mother wanted to run out and look for him, although his father assured her he had hunted everywhere. But Mrs. Petrell said, "If I know anything about Emil, he'll turn up here all right."

She spoke correctly, for at that very moment Emil was walking through her gate. But then he caught sight of something that made him pause. Next door to Mrs. Petrell lived the mayor, in a beautiful house with an orchard surrounding it, and among the apple trees a boy was walking on stilts. It was the mayor's little son, Gottfrid. He caught sight of Emil and went head first into a lilac bush. If you have ever walked on stilts, you will know why. It isn't easy to balance on those long poles with only a little wooden ledge to stand on. But Gottfrid soon sat up and peered at Emil with interest. When two small boys with the same tastes meet for the first time, their eyes light up. Emil and

55

Gottfrid looked at each other and grinned.

"I wish I had a cap like yours," said Gottfrid. "Will you lend it to me?"

"No," said Emil. "I'll borrow your stilts instead."

"All right, but I don't think you'll manage to walk on them," said Gottfrid.

"We'll see," said Emil.

He was more venturesome than Gottfrid had imagined. In an instant he was up on the stilts and off through the apple trees. He had entirely forgotten about lunch with Mrs. Petrell.

But inside the glass veranda the Katthult

folk had finished the fish pie. It hadn't taken long, and now it was time for the blueberry juice. There was plenty of that. A huge bowl, filled to the brim, stood on the table.

"Help yourselves," said Mrs. Petrell. "I hope you've got good appetites."

She herself had no more appetite and didn't touch the juice, but talked all the more. She talked about the great comet, as everyone in Vimmerby was doing that day.

"It would be too appalling," she said, "if a comet should bring the world to an end."

"Yes, who knows, maybe this blueberry juice is the last thing we shall ever eat," said

Emil's mother, and his father hurriedly held out his dish for more.

"May I have a second helping?" he said. "Just to be on the safe side."

But before Mrs. Petrell had time to serve him, something awful happened. There was a crash, a shriek, and an object came through the big glass windows behind Mrs. Petrell, and bits of broken glass and blueberry juice flew all over the veranda.

"The comet!" shrieked Mrs. Petrell, and

she collapsed on the floor in a faint.

But it wasn't the comet. It was only Emil, who came hurtling through the window like a cannonball, and fell headlong into the blueberry juice, which splashed all over the place.

Oh dear, what a to-do there was! Emil's mother screamed, his father roared, and little Ida cried. Only Mrs. Petrell remained quiet, as she lay on the floor in a faint.

"Quick! Fetch cold water from the kitchen," cried Emil's father. "We must moisten her forehead."

Emil's mother hurried off as fast as she could, and his father rushed after her to urge her to go faster.

Emil scrambled out of the tureen, bright blue all over.

"Why are you always in such a hurry for your meals?" asked little Ida, reproachfully. Emil didn't answer.

"Gottfrid was quite right," he said. "You can't climb over a fence on stilts. That's settled, once and for all."

But then he saw poor Mrs. Petrell, lying on the floor, and felt sorry for her.

"Why are they taking so long to fetch a

little water?" he asked. "We've got to hurry."

He wasn't at a loss to know what to do. He seized the blueberry juice bowl and emptied all that remained in it over Mrs. Petrell's face. And believe it or not, that did the trick.

"Blurp!" said Mrs. Petrell, and rose to her feet at once. It shows how useful it is to have lots of blueberry juice in case of emergencies.

"I've cured her already," said Emil, proudly, when at last his parents came running back from the kitchen with water.

But his father looked grimly at him and said, "I know somebody who is going to be cured in the toolshed when we get home."

Mrs. Petrell was still dizzy, and blue in the face, like Emil. But Emil's mother, being quick and resourceful, helped her lie down on a sofa and then got hold of a scrubbing brush.

60

"Now we'll tidy you up," she said, and set to work with the brush, first on Mrs. Petrell, then on Emil, and finally on the floor of the veranda. Soon there was not a trace of blueberry juice to be seen except for a speck on one of Emil's ears. His mother swept up the bits of glass, and his father ran off to a glazier to get a new window which he put in to replace the broken one. Emil wanted to help, but his father wouldn't allow him near it.

"Get away," he hissed. "Clear out and don't come back until it's time for us to go home."

Emil didn't mind disappearing. He was longing to have another talk with Gottfrid. But

he was hungry. He had had nothing except a mouthful of blueberry juice which he managed to gulp while he was in the tureen.

"Have you any food in the house?" he asked Gottfrid, who was standing by the fence in the mayor's garden.

"You bet we have," said Gottfrid. "It's Papa's fiftieth birthday today, and we're having a party. There's lots of food; the larder doors are bursting."

"Goodie," said Emil. "I'd like to try some."

Gottfrid at once went off to the kitchen and returned with masses of good things. Piled on a plate were chipolatas, meatballs, different

kinds of little pasties, and a variety of other things. Then they stood, one on each side of the fence, sharing the eatables, and Emil was very happy.

Presently Gottfrid said, "We're going to have a fireworks display tonight. The biggest there has ever been in Vimmerby."

Poor Emil had never in his life seen fireworks, for such frivolities were never thought of in Lönneberga. It was bitterly mortifying to know he wouldn't be able to see the giant fireworks display, as the Katthult folk would have to return home long before nightfall.

He sighed. When he started to think about it, the Fair had been a poor show altogether. No horse, no fireworks, only misfortunes and a toolshed awaiting him at home. He bade Gottfrid a gloomy farewell and went off to find Alfred, who was his source of comfort in times of distress.

But where was Alfred? The streets were crowded, and finding Alfred in all that hurlyburly wouldn't be easy. He trudged about hunting for hours, and got into several kinds of mischief which were never recorded in any notebook, since nobody knew about them; but he didn't find Alfred.

Twilight comes early in the month of October. Soon it began to get dark, and shortly this Fair Day would be a thing of the past. Market traders were already thinking of going home, and the people of Vimmerby ought also to have begun going indoors, but they didn't want to. They wanted to continue laughing, talking, shouting, and making noise in the streets. They all looked oddly excited—well, think what sort of a day it was! Fair Day, the mayor's birthday, and possibly the last day upon earth, if that comet was really going to strike. When people

are scared and happy at the same time, they make more noise than usual; so the streets were extra turbulent and the houses themselves empty and quiet, with nobody at home except maybe a cat and one or two old grannies who had to look after the babies.

Emil thought it was all very exciting and great fun. He had forgotten his depression and was sure that sooner or later he would find Alfred. And so he did, but first something else happened.

Just as he was passing a little side street he heard a tremendous uproar from a dark backyard. There were men shouting and swearing and a horse neighing. Emil darted through the gate to see what was happening. And what he saw made him jump. There was an old smithy in the yard, and from the light of the furnace Emil saw his horse, his little brown horse, surrounded by a group of angry men. Guess why they were so angry? Because the little brown horse absolutely refused to allow himself to be shod. The moment the blacksmith tried to lift up the horse's leg, he kicked and reared and lashed out in the wildest way, causing the men to scatter in all directions. The blacksmith

pulled his hair and was utterly at a loss to know
what to do.

"I've shod many a horse in my day," he
said, "but I've never come across anything like
this."

The little brown horse had evidently made
up his mind that he didn't want to be shod. He
stood quietly as long as nobody touched his
back leg, but the moment the blacksmith laid a
hand on it, the same thing happened; he kicked
himself loose although there were half a dozen
men trying to hold him. The horse dealer from
Målilla who had bought him became more and
more enraged.

"I'll do it myself," he said at last, and
seized hold of the horse's back leg. But the

horse gave him such a kick that he went flying into a puddle.

"Ah, mark my words," said an old man, who stood watching, "you'll never get that horse shod. They've tried to do it at home in Tuna at least twenty times."

Then the horse dealer realized that he had been tricked, and grew angrier than ever.

"Anyone who likes can have the darned horse," he shouted, "as long as he takes it out of my sight."

And who should come forward then but Emil!

"I'll have him," he said.

The dealer laughed. "You, you cheeky little upstart!"

He hadn't meant that he really wanted to give away the horse, but since so many people had heard him say so, he had to get out of it by some smart argument, so he said, "Very well, you shall have him if you can hold him quiet while he is shod."

Everyone laughed, for they all had tried, and knew that nobody could hold this horse.

But you needn't think Emil was stupid. He knew more about horses than anyone in Lönneberga, indeed in all Småland, and as the little horse kicked and reared and neighed, he thought, that horse behaves just like Lina when I tickled her.

Exactly! Emil was the only person who realized that the little horse was terribly ticklish. That was why he snorted and kicked, just like Lina. And when he neighed so wildly, it was just like Lina, who laughed hysterically when anyone tickled her backbone—well, you yourselves know what it is like to be ticklish.

Emil went up to the horse and held his head between his two strong little hands and said, "Now listen. I'm going to have you shod, and don't make a fuss, for I promise not to tickle you."

Then he went behind the horse and took firm hold of his hoof and held it up. And the horse turned his head placidly around to see what Emil was up to. For a horse has no more feeling in his hoof that you have in your nails, and isn't a bit ticklish there.

"Here you are; come on and shoe him," said Emil to the blacksmith. "I'll hold him."

There was a general stir and murmur among the onlookers, and they went on mutter-

ing as Emil helped the smith to shoe all four hooves.

But when that was done, the horse dealer changed his mind. He didn't want to keep his word about giving away the horse. Instead, he took a bank note out of his wallet and offered it to Emil.

"This will settle matters," he said.

But the onlookers were angry, for they were men of their word.

"Don't try that," they said. "The lad must have the horse."

And so he did. They all knew th was rich, and for his honor's sake he h his promise.

"Oh well, three-hundred kronor won't break me," he said. "Take the horse and clear out."

Just imagine Emil's delight! He jumped onto his newly shod horse and rode out of the gate like a great general. All the countryfolk cheered, and the blacksmith said, "That's the sort of thing that happens at Vimmerby Fair."

Emil rode through the teeming crowds, his face shining with pride and joy, and in the midst of the jostling turmoil he saw Alfred. Alfred stopped dead, opened his eyes very wide, and said, "Bless and save us—whose horse is that?"

"Mine," said Emil. "His name is Lukas, and what do you know he's as ticklish as Lina."

Lina came along at that very moment and tugged on Alfred's sleeve.

"We're going home; the master's just harnessing up."

Yes, now the fun and merrymaking was over and the Katthult folk were off to Lönneberga again. But one thing Emil was determined to do, and that was to show Gottfrid his horse.

"Tell Papa I'll be there in five minutes," he said, and rode off to the mayor's garden at

such a pace that the stones in the road fairly rattled.

The October dusk had settled over the mayor's house and orchard, but all the windows were lit up and talk and laughter sounded from inside the house. The party was in full swing.

Gottfrid didn't care for parties. He was in the garden. He had taken to his stilts again. But he went head over heels into the lilac bushes when he caught sight of Emil on horseback.

"Whose horse is that?" he asked, as soon as he could disentangle his nose from the bushes.

"Mine," answered Emil. "He is mine!"

At first Gottfrid wouldn't believe it, but when he realized it was true, he went quite wild. Hadn't he begged his father for a horse, begging and pleading from morning until night, and

71

what had his father answered every time?

"You're too young. No boy of your age has a horse."

What a complete lie! Here was Emil; his father could come outside and look, and if he had eyes in his head, he could see for himself. But the mayor continued to sit indoors at the table, with lots of stupid people who just ate and drank and chattered on and on and on.

"I can't get him to come out," said Gottfrid, gloomily, his eyes full of tears.

Emil felt sorry for Gottfrid, and he was never at a loss for what to do. If the mayor wouldn't come to the horse, the horse must go to the mayor—it was quite simple. It only meant riding up the steps and through the door, across the hall and into the dining room. All Gottfrid had to do was to open the doors.

If you have ever happened to be at a party when a horse suddenly came in, you will know that people stare and jump up as if they had never seen a horse before. That's what they did at the mayor's party. Especially the mayor. He jumped to his feet, and a bite of cake went down the wrong way, so he couldn't answer when Gottfrid yelled, "What do you say to that?

Now you see that some young chaps have horses!"

Everyone was delighted that a horse had come, because horses are charming animals. They all wanted to pat Lukas. Emil sat on Lukas's back, smiling with happiness. Of course they were welcome to pat his horse.

But then an old major wanted to show how well he understood horses. He wanted to pinch Lukas's back leg—alas, he didn't know how ticklish he was!

The mayor had managed to stop choking on the bite of cake and was going to say something to Gottfrid at the very moment when the major was passing his hand down Lukas's back leg. In the next moment, a pair of hooves flew up and overturned a small table, and a big iced

cream cake went sailing through the air and landed with a splosh right in the mayor's face.

"Blurp!" said the mayor.

Oddly enough, everyone roared with laughter, not knowing any better. Only the mayor's wife didn't laugh. She came anxiously forward with the cake server. A scraping operation was immediately necessary; so that her poor husband would at least have a peephole to see through the cream. Otherwise he would be unable to know what was happening at his birthday party.

Emil suddenly remembered that it was time for him to go back to Lönneberga, and rode hurriedly out the door. Gottfrid came running after him, for it was no good trying to talk to his father when he was covered in cream. Besides, Gottfrid couldn't bear to lose sight of Lukas.

Emil waited outside to say good-bye to him.

"Oh, how lucky you are!" said Gottfrid, giving Lukas a final pat.

"I know I am," said Emil. Gottfrid sighed.

"But we shall have the fireworks display, anyhow," he said, to console himself. "Look!"

He showed Emil all the fireworks lying ready on a garden table in the arbor, and Emil felt a pang. He was in a hurry, but he had never seen a fireworks display in all his life.

"Perhaps I could just set off one," said Emil. "Just to see if there's any zip in them."

Gottfrid didn't hesitate for long, and took one out of the pile.

"Well, just this little jumping jack," he said.

Emil nodded and slid down off the horse's back. "Yes, just this little jumping jack. I'll need a match."

He got one, and pop pop pop, the little sparkling jumping jack darted away—there was certainly "zip" in it. It zigzagged here and there and at last hopped back onto the table among all the other fireworks. It didn't want to be all on its own, I suppose. Neither Emil nor Gottfrid noticed, for all of a sudden they heard a loud voice just behind them. It was the mayor, who had come rushing out onto the steps, wanting to speak to them. He had got rid of nearly all the cream, but his moustache still shone white in the October dusk.

In the streets people still milled about,

75

laughing and shouting, not knowing whether to expect something terrible or something pleasant.

And then it came! The terrifying thing they had been expecting. Suddenly the whole sky caught fire over the mayor's house. The air was full of burning, hissing snakes and glowing clusters and shooting fire that spluttered, fizzed, popped, and spat, causing the people to turn pale with fright, poor things.

"The comet!" they shrieked. "We're all going to be killed!"

And there were cries and screams such as had never been heard before in the town, for everyone thought their last hour had come. Small wonder that they shrieked and fainted in heaps on the streets. Only Mrs. Petrell sat quite calmly in her glass veranda and watched the balls of fire whirling about outside.

"I don't believe in comets anymore," she said to the cat. "I won't mind betting it's that boy Emil up to his pranks again."

She spoke truly. It certainly was Emil and his little jumping jack that had set off all the birthday fireworks at one go, and made all that smoke.

But it was fortunate that the mayor happened to come out at the right moment, or he mightn't have seen any of his beautiful fireworks. Now he stood in the midst of the banging and fizzing, and he had to keep dodging out of the path of each spitting ball of fire which whizzed past his ears. Emil and Gottfrid were sure he was enjoying it because of the little shrill yelps he gave as he skipped from side to side. It was only when a rocket exploded up one of his trouser legs that he must have been annoyed. Why else would he have kicked up such a tremendous fuss and kept yelling as he rushed toward the rainwater butt at the corner of the

house, and frantically thrust his leg down into it? Though you shouldn't do that to rockets, of course; it puts them out. He ought to have known that.

"Well, anyhow I've seen a fireworks display," said Emil, as he lay hidden behind the mayor's woodshed, with Gottfrid beside him.

"Yes, in any event you've seen fireworks," agreed Gottfrid. Then they kept quiet and waited. Not for anything special, but just until the mayor stopped buzzing around the garden like a large, angry bumblebee.

By the time the Katthult waggonette went trundling home later on, all the suns and fiery

clusters had died down, and only the stars were shining above the treetops. The woods and roadway were dark, but Emil was happy and he sang as he rode his horse through the darkness:

Lucky, lucky, lucky me,
See my horse and you'll agree.
Strong and sound in wind and limb,
Never was a horse like him.
When you see him, you'll agree
I'm lucky, lucky, lucky me.

And his father drove along, very pleased with his son. To be sure, Emil had nearly frightened the life out of Mrs. Petrell and the rest of Vimmerby with his tricks. But all the same, hadn't he got the horse for nothing? That made up for everything. There wasn't another lad like him in all of Lönneberga, and this time there was no question of the toolshed.

Besides, Emil's father was in an expansive

mood, for just as he was about to start for home, he had met an old friend who treated him to several bottles of good Vimmerby ale. Not that he usually drank ale, he wasn't that sort of chap, but when it was offered free gratis and for nothing, what could he do? He flourished the whip cheerfully as he drove along, and hiccupped.

"Oho!" said Emil's mother. "It's lucky we don't go to market every day. How nice it will be to get home!"

Little Ida slept in her lap, clutching her Fair Day present, a little china basket decorated with pink china rosebuds, with the words "Souvenir from Vimmerby" printed across it.

In the back seat Lina leaned against Alfred's arm. Alfred's arm was asleep too, for Lina had been hanging on it for a long time. But he himself was wide awake and in the same good spirits as his master, and he said to Emil, who had ridden alongside him, "We'll do some dung spreading all day tomorrow—that will be fine."

"Tomorrow I shall ride my horse all day," said Emil. "That will be fine."

And just then the waggonette rounded the last turn in the road and they could see a light in the kitchen window of Katthult, where Krösa-Maja waited for them with supper.

Perhaps you may think that Emil gave up getting into mischief because he now had a horse, but that wasn't the case. He rode Lukas for three whole days, but by the third day, which was November 3, he was ready to get up to his pranks again. Guess what he did—ha ha, it makes me laugh whenever I think about it. Well, on that particular day he—no! Stop! I promised his mother never to tell what he did on November 3, because soon after that the Lönnebergans collected all that cash, you remember, and wanted to send Emil to America. Emil's mother didn't want to remember it and never even wrote about it in her notebook, so why should I give it away? No, instead you shall hear what Emil did on Boxing Day that year.

MONDAY THE TWENTY-SIXTH OF
DECEMBER, WHEN EMIL MADE A
CLEAN SWEEP IN KATTHULT AND
CAUGHT THE SUPERINTENDENT IN
A WOLF PIT

Before Christmas comes one must face the cold,
windy, dark autumn when there isn't much fun
to be found anywhere. There wasn't much to be
found in Katthult, either. Alfred followed the
oxen in pouring rain and plowed the stony
fields. And Emil trudged after him, helping
Alfred to shout at the oxen, which were slug-
gish and awkward and didn't understand what
plowing was about. But it grew dark early, and
after Alfred had unyoked the oxen, they all
lumbered home. Then Alfred and Emil would
come into the kitchen with great clods of earth

on their boots, and infuriate Lina, who was fussy about her newly scrubbed floor.

"She's so pernickety," said Alfred. "Whoever marries her won't have any peace in his life."

"That will be you," said Emil.

Alfred was thoughtful and silent.

"No, it won't be," he said at last. "I daren't. But I daren't tell her so, either."

"Would you like me to?" asked Emil, who was as bold as brass, but Alfred wouldn't agree to that.

"It's got to be put delicately," he said, "so as not to upset her."

He pondered the matter for a long time, wondering how to tell Lina that he didn't want to marry her, but he couldn't think of a nice way of doing so.

Now the dark autumn days hung heavily over Katthult. The paraffin lamps in the kitchen had to be lit as early as three o'clock in the afternoon, and the family sat there together, doing their various jobs. Emil's mother had a spinning wheel going, and spun fine white wool to make stockings for Emil and Ida. Lina carded the wool, as did Krösa-Maja when she

was there. Emil's father soled shoes, thereby
saving lots of money which the village shoe-
maker would otherwise have had. Alfred was
no less diligent—he mended his own stockings.
They always had enormous holes in the toes and
heels, but Alfred quickly cobbled them together.
Lina would have liked to help him, but Alfred
wouldn't let her.

"No, because then I could be caught," he explained to Emil. "And it wouldn't be any good no matter how delicately I put it."

Emil and Ida often sat under the table, playing with the cat. Once Emil tried to make Ida believe that the cat was really a wolf, and when she wouldn't believe it, he let out a wolf howl which practically made everyone in the kitchen jump out of their skin. His mother wanted to know why he made that noise, and Emil said, "Because there's a wolf under the table."

Krösa-Maja began at once to talk about wolves, and Emil and Ida eagerly came out from under the table to listen to her. She was sure to tell some frightful tales, they knew, for all her stories were frightful. If they weren't about murderers, thieves, ghosts, and spooks, they were about throats being cut, ghastly calamities from fire, appalling tragedies, fatal illnesses, or dangerous beasts. Such as wolves, for instance.

"When I was little," began Krösa-Maja, "there were a great many wolves here in Småland."

"But then Karl XII came and shot them," said Lina.

This made Krösa-Maja angry, for although she was old, she wasn't as old as Lina imagined.

"You show how stupid you are by saying such things," said Krösa-Maja, and refused to go on with her tale. But Emil coaxed her, and at last she started to tell terrible stories of wolves, and how men once dug pits in order to catch them, when she was young.

"So Karl XII didn't need to come, then," began Lina, but checked herself hastily. It was no use; Krösa-Maja was cross again, and small wonder. Karl XII was a king who had lived hundreds of years before, and Krösa-Maja wasn't as old and worn out as all that.

But Emil coaxed her again, and she told them about the werewolves, the most dangerous wolves of all, which only came out when it was

86

moonlight. They could speak, she said, for they weren't actual wolves, but rather something between a wolf and a human being—the most dangerous monsters. If you met one in the moonlight, it was all over for you, because they were worse than any wild beast. "That is why people should stay indoors when it is moonlight," said Krösa-Maja, glaring at Lina.

"Although Karl XII——" began Lina.

Krösa-Maja flung the wool carder away and said she must get home now, as she felt so old and weary.

That night, as Emil and Ida lay in bed, they began talking about wolves again.

"What a good thing there aren't any nowadays," said Ida.

"Aren't any?" said Emil. "How do you

know that, when there are no pits to catch them in?"

He lay awake for a long time thinking about it, and the longer he thought, the more certain he became that if he had a wolf pit, he could catch a wolf in it. And the very next morning he began digging a wolf pit in the ground between the toolshed and the food store. In summertime lots of nettles grew there, but now they lay black and withered on the ground.

It takes a pretty long time to dig a wolf pit, for it must be deep enough to prevent the wolf from escaping after it has fallen in. Alfred helped Emil and took a turn at the digging now and then, but it wasn't until almost Christmastime that the pit was finished.

"But that doesn't matter," said Alfred, "because the wolves won't come out of the woods until the cold winter weather when they are starving."

Little Ida shuddered when she thought of the hungry wolves in the woods, which would come creeping out on cold winter nights and start howling near the house. But Emil didn't shudder. He looked with sparkling eyes at Alfred and was thrilled with the thought of the wolves that would fall into his pit.

"Now I've only got to cover it with twigs and branches so that the wolf won't see where the trap is," he said happily.

"Quite right. 'Cunning is what counts,' as Stolle Jocke said when he caught the flea with his toes," said Alfred.

That used to be a sort of saying in Lönneberga. Alfred shouldn't have quoted it, for Stolle Jocke was his grandfather, who lived in the poorhouse in Lönneberga, and one should never make fun of one's grandfather. But Alfred meant no harm; he only quoted what other folk said.

Then they only had to wait for the cold winter weather, and it came all right. Just before Christmas it turned very cold and began snowing until all of Katthult and Lönneberga

and Småland was one great snowdrift. Only
the tops of the fences stuck up to show where
the road was. And nobody could possibly see
that there was a wolf pit between the toolshed
and the food store.

Now there was hustle and bustle in
Katthult, for they celebrated Christmas there
thoroughly. First of all there was a great wash
day. Lina and Krösa-Maja stood on the icy
jetty by the brook and did the rinsing. Lina
cried and blew on her frozen fingertips which
were very painful. Then they slaughtered the
great Christmas pig, and after that there was

90

scarcely room for anything or anybody else in the kitchen, Lina observed. For there were the black puddings, pork sausages, oatmeal sausages, meat sausages, and potato sausages crammed among bacon, preserves, spareribs of pork, and I don't know what else. Juniper berry juice was brewed by Emil's mother in the brew-

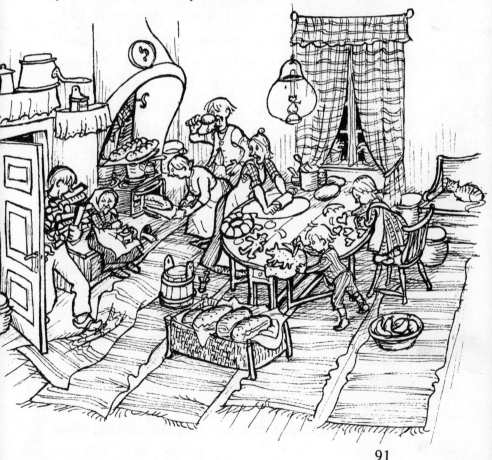

house, in a big wooden vat, for the Christmas celebrations. And enough cakes and bread were baked to make you dizzy—rye bread, malt bread, saffron bread, wheaten bread, gingerbread, and delicious rolls, meringues, and pastries—oh, beyond number. And candles, of course, they had to have them too. Emil's mother and Lina spent almost one entire evening dipping tallow candles, big ones and little ones and special Christmas ones. And Emil and Alfred harnessed Lukas to the wood sledge and went to the woods for a Christmas tree. And Emil's father went to the barn and brought back a couple of sheaves of oats which he had saved for the sparrows. "It's a stupid thing to do," he said, "but after all, the sparrows must have their Christmas."

There were others to think of as well, who had to have a bit of Christmas cheer. All the old paupers in the poorhouse. You won't know what a poorhouse is, for which you ought to be grateful. It is something belonging to olden times, and if I were to tell you all about poorhouses, it would be more terrible than any of Krösa-Maja's frightening tales of murderers and ghosts and wild beasts. Imagine a miserable little tumbledown two-room cottage, where poor, old, worn-out people live together in a state of dirt, vermin, hunger, and wretchedness —then you will know what a poorhouse is, or was. The one in Lönneberga was no worse than others, but it was a horrible place to have to live when poor people grew old and were no longer able to manage for themselves.

"Poor grandfather," Alfred used to say, "his life isn't very happy. It wouldn't be so bad if it weren't for the superintendent."

The superintendent was the person in charge of the poorhouse. She was a pauper herself, but she was the biggest and strongest and worst tempered one, and so had been given charge of the poorhouse. This ought never to have happened, and wouldn't have, if Emil had

been grown up and president of the local council. But now he was only a little boy, and could do nothing about the superintendent. Alfred's grandfather was afraid of her, and so were all the other paupers, too.

"She goes about like a roaring lion in the sheepfold," Stolle Jocke used to say. He was a little queer in the head and used to talk as if he were reading the Bible, but he was a dear old man and Alfred was fond of him.

The people living in the poorhouse hardly ever got a proper meal, which was shocking, Emil's mother considered.

"Poor things, they shall have something for Christmas," she said. Which was why Emil and Ida were seen, a couple of days before Christmas, plodding up the snowy road towards the poorhouse carrying a big basket between them. Emil's mother had filled it with all sorts of good things. There were sausages of different kinds, bacon, ham, rye loaves, black puddings, saffron buns, gingerbread, candles, and a little paper twist of snuff for Stolle Jocke.

Only those who have gone hungry themselves for a long time can understand how glad the poor people were when Emil and Ida came

in with their basket. They all wanted to begin
eating at once, but the superintendent said,
"Not until Christmas Eve—you know that
quite well." And nobody dared disagree.

Emil and Ida went back home, and the
next day was Christmas Eve. In Katthult, that
day was great fun and so was Christmas Day
itself. They all went to the early service in
Lönneberga church. Emil beamed with happiness as he drove in the basket sleigh, for Markus
and Lukas ran so fast that the snow whirled
around their hooves, leaving all the other sleighs
far behind.

Emil sat quiet and still during the whole
service, behaving so well that his mother wrote
in the blue notebook, "The boy is really pious

and didn't get up to any mischief in church, at all events."

All through that long Christmas Day Emil was equally well behaved. He and Ida played happily with their presents, and peace reigned over all of Katthult.

But then came Boxing Day, when Emil's parents were to go to a party in Skorphult, which lay on the farther side of the parish. Emil was known too well, so the children were not invited.

"I don't mind," said Emil, "but it's hard luck on the Skorphult folk, because at that rate they'll never meet me."

"Nor me," said Ida.

It had been arranged for Lina to stay behind and look after the children that day. But she had begun grumbling early that morning and clamored to be allowed to visit her mother, who lived in a croft near Skorphult. She thought how nice it would be to ride in the sledge, as her employers were going in that direction, anyway.

"Oh, I can look after the children," said Alfred. "There's food aplenty, and I can see to it that they don't play with matches, or anything of that sort."

"Well, you know what Emil's like," said Emil's father, staring gloomily before him.

But his mother said, "Emil's a good little chap. He doesn't get into mischief at Christmastime, anyway. Don't grizzle, Lina, you shall come with us."

And so it was settled. Alfred and Emil and Ida stood at the kitchen window and watched the sleigh disappear over the hill, and when it was out of sight, Emil capered with delight.

"Hurrah! Now for some fun!" he cried.

But then little Ida pointed toward the road.

"Here comes Stolle Jocke," she said.

"So he does," said Alfred. "What's wrong, I wonder."

Stolle Jocke, you see, wasn't allowed out. He was a bit simple and unable to look after himself, or so the superintendent said.

"He'd get lost, and I haven't time to run about and hunt for him."

But he found his way to Katthult, anyhow, and now he was coming along the road like a little shriveled bit of leather, with his white hair fluttering around his ears. Soon he was standing inside the kitchen door.

"We haven't had any black pudding," he

sobbed, "and no sausages, either. The superintendent has taken it all."

He was crying so hard that he couldn't say anything else.

Emil was so enraged, so terribly angry that Alfred and Ida scarcely dared look at him. His eyes were wild, and he seized a porcelain bowl from the table. He flung it at the wall, and it smashed to smithereens.

"Give me my gun!" he yelled.

Alfred became really alarmed.

"Calm down, for goodness sake," he said. "It's dangerous to get into such a temper."

Then Alfred began soothing and comforting his poor grandfather, and wanted to know why the superintendent had behaved so badly. But all Jocke could say was, "We haven't had any black pudding. And no sausages, either. And I didn't get my sn-u-u-ff," he sobbed.

Then Ida pointed along the road again. "Look," she said. "Here comes Lillklossan."

"To take me home," said Jocke, beginning to tremble.

Lillklossan was a little woman from the poorhouse whom the superintendent used to send to Katthult whenever Jocke disappeared. It was generally to Katthult that he came, for Alfred and Emil's mother were there, and she was always so kind to poor people.

From Lillklossan they heard what had happened. The superintendent had hidden the food up in the attic in a cupboard. But on Christmas

Eve, when she went to take it out, there was one wretched little sausage missing, and she was wild with rage.

"Like a raging lion in the sheepfold," said Jocke, and Lillklossan agreed with him. Goodness gracious, what a fuss she had kicked up over that sausage, and she meant to make the sinner confess to having stolen it.

"Otherwise there'll be a Christmas that will make the angels weep," she said. And Lillklossan confirmed this. Because nobody would admit to having stolen the sausage, however much she raved and shouted. Some of them thought the superintendent was making the affair an excuse for keeping all the good things for herself, but in any event they had had a Christmas that would make the angels weep, said Lillklossan. The superintendent had sat up in her attic room, with the candles alight, eating sausages, blood pudding, ham, and saffron buns until she was fit to burst, the fat old beast. But down below, the rest of them sat along the walls and cried, and only had a little salt herring to eat, even though it was Christmas Eve.

And it was the same thing on Christmas Day. The superintendent swore that nobody should have as much as half a blood pudding until the sausage thief came forward and confessed. And until that happened, she sat up there eating and eating and speaking to nobody. Lillklossan had peeped at her through the keyhole about once an hour, and had seen all the good things that Emil's mother had sent disappearing into her gaping mouth. But now she was scared that Jocke had gone to Katthult to tell on her, and she had told Lillklossan over and over again to bring him back for heaven's sake.

"So now we'd better go at once, Jocke," said Lillklossan.

"Yes, poor Grandfather," said Alfred. "Life is hard for the poor."

Emil said nothing. He sat on the log box gritting his teeth. He went on sitting there, thinking, long after Jocke and Lillklossan had disappeared. At last he struck his fist on the log box, and said, "I know someone who is going to give a party!"

"Who is?" asked Ida.

Emil thumped his fist on the box again.

"I am," he said. And he explained his plan. There was going to be a party as never before imagined, for every single one of the paupers from the poorhouse was to come to Katthult without further delay.

"Yes, but, Emil," said Ida anxiously, "are you sure that won't be getting into mischief?"

Alfred, too, was worried about the same thing, but Emil assured them it would be nothing of the sort. It would be a good deed, over which God's angels would clap their hands for joy, just as hard as they had previously wept because of the poorhouse's miserable Christmas.

"And Mama will be pleased, too," said Emil.

"But what about Papa?" asked Ida.

"Hmm," said Emil. "But it isn't naughty, anyway." Then he relapsed into silence and began thinking again. "But to get the lion out of the sheepfold, that'll be the trickiest part," he said. "Come on, we'll go there and try."

As well as stuffing herself with the sausages, black puddings, bacon, all the saffron buns, and gingerbread, the superintendent had carefully sniffed up every grain of Jocke's snuff. Now she sat in her attic and felt miserable, as one does when one has done wrong by eating far too much black pudding. She wouldn't go

102

down to the others, for they only glared at her and sighed and wouldn't say a word.

But as she sat there, she heard someone knocking at the downstairs door, and hurried down the attic stairs as fast as she could to see who it was.

It was Emil. And that worried her, for supposing Jocke or Lillklossan had told tales, and Emil had come on that account.

But Emil bowed politely, and said, "Did I happen to leave my clasp knife here, when I came?"

Just think how smart Emil was! His clasp knife was safe and sound in his pocket, but he had to make some excuse for coming. The superintendent assured him that they hadn't seen any knife. Then Emil said, "Were the sausages nice? And the bacon and other things?"

The superintendent looked down at her broad feet and said, hurriedly, "Oh yes, yes, your dear mother knows what the paupers need. Thank her very much."

Then Emil said what he had come there to say, but he did so offhandedly, and as if it were not important. "Mama and Papa have gone to a party in Skorphult."

The superintendent grew very excited. "Is there a party in Skorphult today? I didn't know."

No, or you'd have been off there ages ago, thought Emil, who, like everybody else in Lönneberga, knew that whenever there was a party the superintendent would turn up at the kitchen door, as regular as clockwork. And it would be impossible to get rid of her until she had had a bite of cheesecake, at least. She would go through fire and water for cheesecake.

"Cheesecakes—what do you say to that?" said Emil. He wouldn't tell a lie and didn't know whether they had cheesecakes at Skorphult, so he merely said, cunningly, "What do you say to cheesecakes, eh?"

Then he went away. He had done what he intended. He knew that within half an hour the superintendent would be on her way to Skorphult. And he had reckoned aright. He and Alfred and Ida stood waiting behind the woodshed, and saw the superintendent come out, wrapped in her warmest woolen shawl, with her begging bag under her arm, on her way to Skorphult. But just imagine what a disaster! She locked the door and tucked the key into the bag—what a fine thing! Now they were trapped as though in a prison, poor paupers, and the superintendent was glad about that. Should Stolle Jocke try to run away again, he would see she had the upper hand and was not to be trifled with. So off she trudged to Skorphult, as fast as her fat legs would carry her.

Emil rattled the door and felt how firmly

it was locked. So did Alfred and little Ida—it was fastened securely, there was no doubt about that.

All the paupers clustered at the window and stared in alarm at the three people outside who were trying to get in. But Emil shouted, "You shall have a party at Katthult if we can manage to get you out."

The folk in the poorhouse began buzzing like bees in a hive. It was an unforeseen wonder and delight, but at the same time a grievous calamity, for they were locked in and could see no possibility of getting out.

You will perhaps ask why they didn't open the window and climb out. That shows you have never heard of inner windows. No window could ever be opened in wintertime in the poorhouse because of the double windows. They were nailed up and pasted over with paper to prevent the wind from blowing through the cracks.

But how could anyone breathe, perhaps you may ask? Dear children, how can you ask such a foolish question? Who says anyone needed to breathe fresh air in the poorhouse? Nobody was interested in such foolishness, for

nobody needed more fresh air than that which
came through the open stove and the cracks in
the ramshackle walls and the floor.

Then they couldn't get out of the window,
poor things? Well, there was one window that
opened, but it was in the superintendent's attic.
And no pauper, however hungry, could jump
four metres to get to a party, for that would be
jumping straight into Heaven, for certain.

But Emil didn't give up over trifles. He
fetched a ladder which was hidden behind the
woodshed, and stood it against the superinten-

dent's window, which Jocke had joyfully opened. Alfred climbed up the ladder. He was big and strong, and could carry thin little paupers as easily as anything. Of course, they squealed and groaned, but they all got out. Except Salia Amalia. She didn't dare, and wouldn't come. But Vibergskan promised to

bring back all the food she could from the party, and Amalia was satisfied.

Had anyone been passing along the Katthult road on that Boxing Day as it was getting dark, they would have thought that a line of gray ghosts was limping, swaying, and panting up the hill towards Katthult. And certainly the poor paupers did look ghostly in their rags, but they were happy as larks and as excited as children—oh dear, it was so long since they had been to a Christmas party. It delighted them,

too, to think of the superintendent shortly coming back to an empty poorhouse with only one pauper remaining in it.

"Tee hee hee, she won't have any paupers there and how will she like that?" tittered Johan Ett Öre.

And they all laughed with glee. But when they came into the festive kitchen at Katthult, they grew silent. For Emil had lit five great candles which threw their light on the newly polished copper bowls on the walls, so that everything shone and glittered, and Jocke thought he was in Heaven.

"Ah, here all is light and blessings abounding," he said, and wept, because he always cried as much when he was happy as when he was sad.

Then Emil said, "Now for the feast!"

And feast they did. Emil and Alfred and

little Ida all helped to fetch from the larder as much as they could carry. And I should like you to know what was set on the kitchen table of Katthult that Boxing Day, when they had brought it in.

A dish of black pudding
A dish of pork sausages
A dish of liver paste
A dish of headcheese
A dish of meatballs
A dish of veal cutlets
A dish of spareribs of pork
A dish of oatmeal sausages
A dish of potato sausages
A dish of salmagundi
A dish of salt beef
A dish of ox tongue
A huge ham
A dish of cheesecake
A plate of rye bread
A plate of syrup bread
A crate of juniper berry drinks
A can of milk
A bowl of rice pudding
A bowl of cream cheese
A dish of preserved plums

An apple pie
A jug of cream
A jug of strawberry juice
A jug of pear ginger
And a suckling pig garnished with sugar.

111

And they all sat around the table, those little paupers from the poorhouse, waiting very patiently, but their eyes filled with tears as each dish was brought in.

At last Emil said, "Help yourselves."

And help themselves they did, and they ate and ate.

Alfred and Emil and little Ida ate too, but Ida could only manage a couple of meatballs, for she had begun to think. She was wondering whether, after all, this would count as mischief. And she suddenly remembered that tomorrow all the relatives from Ingatorp were coming to Katthult. And all the party food was vanishing. She heard the chomping and crunching and lip smacking and guzzling all around the table. It was as though a herd of beasts of prey had flung themselves at the bowls and dishes and plates. She realized that people ate like that when they were famished, and it was dreadful. She tugged at Emil's arm and whispered so that only he could hear, "Are you sure this isn't wrong? Think of them coming from Ingatorp tomorrow."

"They're all fat enough already at Ingatorp," said Emil. "It's better to use the food where it does most good."

All the same he began getting rather anxious, because it didn't look as though there was going to be more than half a black pudding left when the feast was over. What wasn't stuffed into their mouths was thrust into their pockets and bags, and dishes were emptied in a flash.

"Here goes the last of the spareribs of pork," said Kalle Spader, and finished the last mouthful.

"And I've finished up the salmagundi," said Rackare-Fia.

"We've made a clean sweep of everything," said Tok Niklas at last, and a truer word was never spoken. That was why this particular party was always known as the Grand Clean Sweep at Katthult, for you must know that they talked about it long afterwards, both in Lönneberga and other parishes.

Only one thing was left, now, and that was the roast suckling pig. It stood on the table and stared sadly with its sugar eyes.

"Ooh, that pig looks like a little spook," said Rackare-Fia. "I'd never dare touch him."

She had never seen a roast suckling pig before, nor had any of the others, and they were

half scared of this one and didn't touch it.

"There isn't another sausage left, by any chance?" said Kalle Spader. But Emil said that in all of Katthult, only one sausage was left, and that was on a twig sticking out of his wolf pit. It was bait for the wolf he was waiting for, so Kalle Spader couldn't have it, nor could anyone else.

This jogged Viberg's memory. "Salia Amalia!" she cried. "We've forgotten her!" She looked all around, and her eyes fastened on the pig.

"Can she have that? Even if it does look like a spook? What do you say, Emil?"

"Yes, she can have it," said Emil with a sigh.

Now they were all so full they couldn't move, and it would have been impossible for them to get back to the poorhouse on their own.

114

"We'll take the wood sledge," said Emil. They had a wood sledge at Katthult, a great clumsy thing which would hold as many paupers as required, even if they were a trifle fatter than usual.

Now evening had come, and the sky burned with stars. There was a full moon, too, and fresh snow and beautiful mild air, a lovely evening for sledging.

Emil and Alfred helped them all up into the sledge. In front sat Vibergskan, with the pig, then all the others from the poorhouse, and finally in the back little Ida, with Alfred and Emil.

"Off we go!" shouted Emil. And off they went, down the hill at a great rate, and they all screamed with delight, for it was so long since they had gone sledging. Only the pig was silent,

staring like a ghost in the moonlight.

And the superintendent? Well, you shall hear about her. I wish you could have seen her when she returned from her cheesecake trip to Skorphult. See how she comes in her gray woolen shawl, fat and complacent, how she takes out the key and puts it into the lock. She chuckles a little when she thinks how meek and submissive all the paupers will be—ha ha! They must learn who's top dog. And now she turns the key and steps over the threshold—but why is it so silent? Are they asleep already? Or are they just sitting around sulking? The moon shone through the window and lit up every corner, so why couldn't she see a living soul? Because nobody was there! No, superintendent, not a living soul!

She began trembling in every limb and was more frightened than she had ever been in her life. Who can get through a locked door? Only God's angels in Heaven—and so it must have been. The poor wretches whom she had robbed of their sausages and black puddings and snuff, had been taken by God's angels to a better place than the poorhouse. Only she herself was left in misery and wretchedness, alas, alas! She

116

howled like a dog.

Then a voice sounded from one of the beds, where a small, pathetic creature lay hidden under the coverlet. "Why are you howling?" asked Salia Amalia.

How quickly the superintendent recovered herself! She bullied Salia Amalia into telling her the whole story. The superintendent was like that.

And then she went hurrying off to Katthult. She had to get her paupers back home, quickly and quietly; so that there wouldn't be too much gossip about the affair in Lönneberga.

Katthult lay lovely in the moonlight. She saw the kitchen window brilliantly lit up. And suddenly she felt too ashamed to go in. She would peep in through the window, first, to make sure that it really was her paupers sitting there and having a feast. But she would need a box, or something of the sort, to stand on, or she wouldn't be able to see in. She turned toward the woodshed to try to find something. And she did find something. But not a box. She found a sausage. Fancy, there was a nice little sausage stuck on a twig in the snow, in the moonlight! She was full to bursting with cheesecake, at the moment, but she knew how quickly one could become hungry again, and to let a whole sausage go by would be too idiotic, she thought. She took a long stride forward. One last long step.

Just at the precise moment that the superintendent fell into the wolf pit, all the paupers came out from Katthult, for the feast was over, and got on the sledge to go home. They didn't hear a sound from the pit, because at first the superintendent wouldn't call for help. She thought she would be able to scramble out, so she kept quiet.

Meanwhile her paupers sped down the hill to the poorhouse, and found, strangely enough, that the door was open. So they went in and tottered to bed, giddy with all the food and the sledging, but happier than they had been for many a long year.

And home to Katthult went Alfred and Emil and little Ida, in the moonlight and star-shine. Emil and Alfred pulled the sledge. Ida rode in it because she was so little.

If ever you have chanced to be out on your sledge on such a calm, moonlit evening in Lönneberga, you will know how oddly silent it is, almost as though the whole world were asleep. So you can imagine how terrifying it would be to hear the most awful howl breaking the silence. As Emil and Alfred and Ida came up the last hill, they suddenly heard a howl from the direction of Emil's wolf trap, a howl that was enough to freeze the blood. Ida turned pale and longed to be with her mother, but Emil didn't. He leapt into the air with delight.

"A wolf has gotten into my trap," he screamed. "Oh, where is my gun?"

But Alfred said, "There's something queer about the sound of that wolf. Listen!"

And they stood still in the moonlight, listening to the eerie howling.

"Help! Help! Help!"

Emil's eyes sparkled. "A werewolf!"

119

He rushed ahead of the others, and reached the pit. And there he saw what kind of wolf he had trapped. Not a werewolf at all, but that horrible superintendent. Emil was furious; what business had she in his pit? He wanted a *real* wolf. But then he reflected. Perhaps it was right that the superintendent should have stumbled into the trap. Perhaps one might tame her a bit, so that she would become gentler and not so ill-tempered. Yes, it would be a way of teaching her manners, because she was certainly in need of such a lesson. So he called to Alfred and Ida, "Come here! Come and look at this ugly, shaggy old beast!"

And they all stood staring down at the superintendent, who did look something like a wolf, in her gray woolen shawl.

"Are you certain that it's a werewolf?"

asked little Ida in a quavering voice.

"Of course it is," said Emil. "An angry old she-werewolf is what this is—the most dangerous kind of all."

"Yes, for they are so greedy," said Alfred.

"Yes, look at her," said Emil. "She's guzzled a lot in her time. But that's at an end now. Alfred, get me my gun."

"No, no! Oh, Emil, don't you see who it is?" shrieked the superintendent, for she was terrified out of her wits when Emil spoke of his gun. She didn't know, of course, that it was just a toy one Alfred had made for Emil.

"Did you hear what the werewolf said, Alfred?" asked Emil. "I didn't."

Alfred shook his head. "I didn't, either," he said.

"Anyway, it doesn't matter. Get me my gun, Alfred," said Emil.

Then the superintendent screamed, "Don't you see it is *I* who am caught down here?"

"What does she say? Get me my gun, Alfred," repeated Emil.

The superintendent began howling at the top of her voice. "You are wicked, all of you!" she sobbed.

"Is she saying she likes black pudding?" asked Emil.

"Yes, that's right," said Alfred. "But we haven't any."

"No, there's none left in all Småland," said Emil. "Because the superintendent gobbled it all up."

Then the superintendent began howling louder than ever, for she realized that Emil knew how badly she had treated Stolle Jocke and the other poor folk. She cried so much that Emil felt sorry for her, for he was a kind-hearted lad. But to make sure that things would improve in the poorhouse, she mustn't be let off too lightly, so he said, "I say, Alfred, if you look more closely at this werewolf, don't you think she is a little like the superintendent at the poorhouse?"

"Oh," said Alfred, "the superintendent is worse than all the werewolves in Småland."

"Yes," agreed Emil, "werewolves are little pets compared to the superintendent. She begrudges everyone anything. I wonder who took that sausage out of the cupboard."

"I did!" shrieked the superintendent. "I did! I'll admit anything you like if only you'll help me get out of this."

Then Alfred and Emil looked at each other and smiled, quietly.

"Alfred," said Emil, "haven't you eyes in your head? Don't you see that it *is* the superintendent, and no werewolf?"

"Why, bless me," said Alfred, "how did we come to make such a mistake?"

"I can't think," said Emil. "Of course, they are alike, but no werewolf has a shawl like that."

"No, that's true, but they do have mohair ones, don't they?"

"Now, Alfred, you must be kind to the superintendent," said Emil. "Fetch a ladder."

So they put a ladder down into the pit, and she climbed up, blubbering, and ran off, for now she wanted to be free of Katthult forever. Never would she set foot there again. But before disappearing she turned around, and called, "I did take the sausage, God forgive me, but I forgot about it on Christmas Eve. I swear I had forgotten about it."

"Well, it was a good thing for her to sit here a bit and remember," said Emil. "Wolf traps aren't such a bad idea after all."

The superintendent hurried down the hill as fast as her fat legs would carry her, and was out of breath when she reached the poorhouse. All the paupers were asleep in their verminous beds, and she wouldn't have woken them up for the world. So, moving more softly than she ever had, she crept in like a ghost.

There they were, safe and sound, all her paupers, and she counted them like sheep. But suddenly she saw something else. On the table, beside Salia Amalia's bed was—oh horrors, a ghost. It was surely a ghost, although it looked like a pig, a dreadful little moonshine pig, or maybe it was a werewolf, standing there staring at her with frightful white eyes!

So many fearful things happening all on the same day were too much for the superintendent. She sank to the ground, with a sigh. And there she lay, not stirring until the sun shone through the windows of the poorhouse on the third day of Christmas.

That was the day when the Ingatorp relations were to come to Katthult for a party—oh dear, what sort of festivities could there be? Well, anyway, there was salt pork out in the food store, and fried pork and potatoes and onion sauce is food fit for a king.

But when Emil's mother wrote in her notebook, she was sad, one must admit, and the page is stained as though somebody had shed tears over it.

"Third Day of Christmas, in my distress about the evening," the entry was headed. And then "The poor child has spent the whole day in the toolshed. He really does mean well, though sometimes I think he is rather crazy."

But life went on in Katthult. Soon the winter was over, and it was springtime. Emil was often shut into the toolshed, but when he wasn't, he played with Ida, rode Lukas and drove the milk float, teased Lina and talked to

125

Alfred, and thought up fresh mischief, which enriched his life and filled it from morning to night. By the month of May he had one-hundred and twenty-five little wooden men on the shelf in the shed—diligent lad!

Alfred didn't get into mischief, but he had his worries, for he hadn't dared to talk to Lina about not wanting to marry her.

"It would be best for me to tell her," said Emil, but Alfred wouldn't hear of it.

"It must be put delicately, I tell you, so as not to upset her."

Alfred was a kindly soul and couldn't think of any possible way of coming out with the truth to Lina. But one Saturday at the beginning of May, as Lina sat on the back door step, obstinately waiting for him to come and canoodle with her, Alfred decided that the time had come. And he leaned out of the window of his bedroom and called to her, "Hey, Lina, there's something I've been wanting to say to you for a long time."

Lina giggled, expecting at last to hear what she had been longing for.

"What is it, then, Alfred dear?" she cooed. "What is it you want to say?"

"Well, it's this business of getting married that we've talked about. It's—it's—it's—well, a lot of codswallop!"

Poor Alfred, it is dreadful to have to say that sort of thing. I really oughtn't to tell you about it, for I don't want to teach you more shocking words than you know already. But you must remember that Alfred was only a poor farmhand in Lönneberga, not someone like you. He couldn't think of a more delicate way of putting it, and he had been brooding over it for so long, poor fellow.

However, Lina wasn't distressed. "Oh, you think so, do you?" she said. "We'll see about that." And he realized at that moment that he would never get rid of Lina. But just that evening he wanted to be free to enjoy himself, so he went with Emil down to the lake, and they fished for perch.

It was a glorious evening of the kind you only get in Småland; all the hedges were in bloom, blackbirds sang, mosquitos hummed, and the perch were biting well. Alfred and Emil sat there and saw their float bob on the shining water. They didn't talk much, but were very happy, all the same. They stayed till the sun began going down, and then went home, Alfred with the perch on a string and Emil playing the pipe Alfred had made for him from a willow twig. Through the field they went, along a winding path under the springtime green of the birches. Emil surprised the blackbird by playing his pipe, but suddenly he stopped and said, "Do you know what I'm going to do tomorrow?"

"No," said Alfred. "Some fresh bit of mischief?"

Emil put the pipe to his mouth and began playing again. He played for a time, and thought hard.

"I don't know," he said at last. "I never know till afterwards."